For Henri

© 2010 l'école des loisirs, Paris, as *Gros Pipi*

This edition published in 2012 by
Eerdmans Books for Young Readers,
an imprint of Wm. B. Eerdmans Publishing Co.
2140 Oak Industrial Dr. NE
Grand Rapids, Michigan 49505
P.O. Box 163, Cambridge CB3 9PU U.K.

www.eerdmans.com/youngreaders

12 13 14 15 16 17 18   10 9 8 7 6 5 4 3 2 1

Manufactured at Tien Wah Press
in Singapore, February 2012, first printing

Library of Congress Cataloging-in-Publication Data

Jadoul, Émile.
All by myself! / by Émile Jadoul.
p. cm.
Summary: Leon Penguin gets up in the middle of the night all by himself to go to the bathroom.
ISBN 978-0-8028-5411-7
[1. Penguins — Fiction. 2. Toilet training — Fiction.] I. Title.
PZ7.J153195All 2012
[E] — dc23
2011049537

The illustrations were rendered in black graphite pencil and oil painting.
The display and text type were set in Romana.

Émile Jadoul

All by Myself!

Eerdmans Books for Young Readers
Grand Rapids, Michigan • Cambridge, U.K.

Every night, it's the same.

Leon wakes up.
He has to use the bathroom.
So Leon calls to his mom:
"Mommy, I need to go *potty!*"

Mommy Penguin gets up
and takes Leon to the bathroom.

And then Mommy and Leon
go back to bed.

Often Leon needs to use the bathroom twice during the night.
So Leon calls to his dad:
"Daddy, I need to go *potty!*"

Daddy Penguin gets up
and takes Leon to the bathroom.
And then Daddy and Leon go back to bed.

Every morning, it's the same.
Mommy and Daddy are very, very tired.

When night comes, Mommy Penguin tells Leon:
"You know what, my sweet Leon? At night,
big boys like you go potty on their own.
Will you try?"

"Well, okay . . ." Leon replies.

That night, Leon wakes up.
He needs to go potty.
He gets up, then hesitates.
What about calling his mom . . . just this once?
He keeps hesitating.
And then, he makes up his mind.

He goes potty . . .

All by himself!

Leon is proud — so proud.

"Daddy, Mommy, wake up!" Leon shouts.
"I'm a big boy now!

I went potty . . .
all by myself!"